The Fable of the Oum Bsisi

The Mouse and the Swallow
A Traditional Libyan Fable

Laila ElOrfi
Illustration: Sara ElOrfi
Co-Illustrator: Darlee Urbiztondo

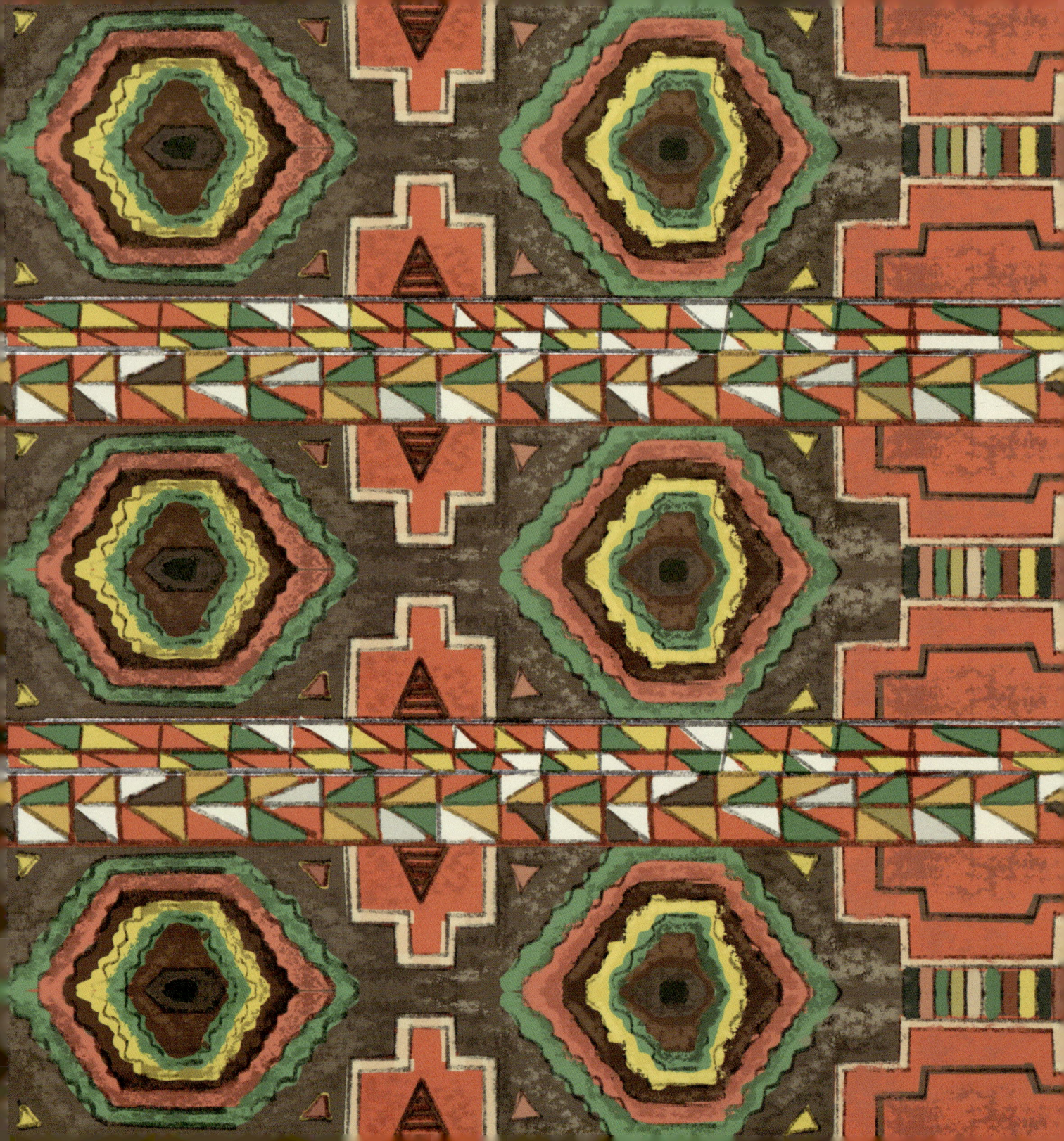

Dedication

My dear father -Mailud Hassan ElOrfi- told me the fable of the Oum Bsisi during my childhood. The story was first narrated by his mother, my late grandmother Hawa Zayed El-Hadadi, who lived in my imagination telling this story to my father when he was a little boy in a place and time far different from my place and time. In today's world overwhelmed by technology, I wanted to share this version of the Libyan traditional story shared by my father, from my memory to my parents, my sons, my nieces, and your children. And if the natural course of life is to move forward, then heritage is worth returning to… through this book we return to the times of Oum Bsisi.

Laila ElOrfi

nce upon a time, the night before Eid, a little mouse asked his mother for some Eid cookies.

"Mother, can you make me some Eid cookies?" the mouse asked.

"Oh, I would love to. But I don't have a flour sifter. Please go to our neighbor, Aunty Oum Bsisi, and ask to borrow her sifter. Then, I'll make the cookies for Eid," Mother suggested.

Oum Bsisi: The local name given to the swallow (bird) in Libya.
Eid: A religious holiday celebrated by Muslims worldwide that marks the end of the month-long dawn-to-sunset fasting of Ramadan

Excitedly, the mouse went over to his neighbor's house. "Aunty Oum Bsisi, I'm your neighbor. My mother sent me to borrow your sifter."

h, please come in child. You'll find the sifter in the kitchen. I have it covering the milk.
But don't touch the milk," added Oum Bsisi in a serious tone.

"Yes, Aunty!" said the mouse.
The mouse went to the kitchen and took the sifter off the milk.

And then he took a sip of the milk!

s he was leaving the house, the swallow called out to him, "Come closer."

When he got closer to her, she saw the milk dripping off his whiskers. She was very angry. "Come a little closer still," urged the swallow.

When he did just that, the swallow attacked him with her beak.
The mouse ran away but she caught him by the tail. And then, she cut his tail right off!

The mouse ran off with the sifter. He cried out to his mother, "Mother, Oum Bsisi has cut off my tail!" Mother felt very sorry for the little mouse. She was so sad. And so, she went to visit the swallow.

My neighbor, Oum Bsisi, why did you cut off my son's tail?
The Eid celebration is tomorrow morning.

Now how can my child play with the other children with a cut tail?
Give it back to me and I will sew it on."

Oum Bsisi answered, "I'm keeping the tail until you replace the milk that your child drank."
"Oh, where can I find milk for you?" Mother asked.

"Go find the goat. She will have milk for you to bring to me, and then I will give you the tail back in return," the swallow explained.

The mouse's mother told her son to go find the goat and ask her for the milk, to be given to Oum Bsisi, and then Oum Bsisi would return his tail.

So, off went the mouse to find the goat. "Aunt Goat, can you please give me some milk? The milk is for Oum Bsisi, and she in return will give me back my tail, so I can play with my friends on the morning of Eid."

The goat said, "I'll give you the milk, but first, get me some Nabaq fruit from the Sidra tree so I can eat and produce milk."

Nabaq fruit: buckthorn; a small deciduous tree or large shrub that can grow to six meters in height. It has dull, green, oval or egg-shaped leaves.

So, off went the mouse to find the Sidra tree. He pleaded, "Oh, Sidra tree, would you please give me some Nabaq fruit? The Nabaq is for the goat, and the goat can give me milk, and the milk is for Oum Bsisi, and she in return will give me back my tail, so I can play with my friends on the morning of Eid."

The Sidra told him, "I'll give you some Nabaq fruit, but first, I need water. Go and bring me water from the stream in the valley."

Sidra tree: also known as the lote tree, or jujube. Its scientific name is ziziphus spina; it is an ancient tree that grows in dry environments.

So, off went the mouse to find the stream in the valley. "Oh, Valley, please give me water for the Sidra tree, so it can give me some Nabaq fruit, and the Nabaq is for the goat, and the goat can give me milk, and the milk is for Oum Bsisi, and she will in return give me back my tail, so I can play with my friends on the morning of Eid."

The Valley answered, "I will give you water, but I need the sound of the Ululators for the rain, to fill the stream, so you can get the water you need. Go to the Bedouin hamlet and ask the Ululators to help you."

To ululate: to utter a loud, usually protracted, high-pitched, rhythmical sound especially as an expression of joy, celebration.

So, off went the mouse to find the bedouin hamlet.

"Oh, dear people of the hamlet, can I please have some help from the Ululators, the valley needs their sound to get water, and the water is for the Sidra tree, and the Sidra tree would give me some Nabaq fruit, and the Nabaq is for the goat, and the goat can give me milk, and then the milk is for Oum Bsisi, and she will in return give me back my tail so I can play with my friends on the morning of Eid."

The Ululators agreed to help on one condition. They wanted a proper meal of lamb. "Go, little mouse, to the shepherd," they ordered. "Then, ask him for a lamb."

So, off went the mouse to find the shepherd. "Mr. Shepherd, can you please give me a lamb for the Ululators? The Ululators will ululate for the valley, and the valley will give me water, and the water is for the Sidra tree, and the Sidra tree would give me some Nabaq fruit, and the Nabaq is for the goat, and the goat can give me milk, and the milk is for Oum Bsisi, and she will in return give me back my tail, so I can play with my friends on the morning of Eid."

The shepherd said he could help, however, he stated, "I need a puppy to help with shepherding my herd. Can you go to the dog? She has a pack of puppies, perhaps she can help."

So, off went the mouse, to find the dog, and he asked her, "Can you please lend me a puppy to help the shepherd? And the shepherd will give me a lamb, and the lamb is for the Ululators, the Ululators will ululate for the valley, and the valley will give me water, and the water is for the Sidra tree, and the Sidra tree would give me some Nabaq fruit, and the Nabaq is for the goat, and the goat can give me milk, and the milk is for Oum Bsisi, and she will in return give me back my tail, so I can play with my friends on the morning of Eid."

The dog said, "My puppies and I can go help out the shepherd, but we are quite hungry. Please bring us some meat from the butcher, so we can eat."

So, off went the mouse to find the butcher. Mr. Butcher, can you please give me some meat to give to the dog and her puppies? And they can help the shepherd, and the shepherd will give me a lamb, and the lamb is for the Ululators, the Ulutators will ululate for the valley, and the valley will give me water, and the water is for the Sidra tree, and the Sidra tree would give me some Nabaq fruit, and the Nabaq is for the goat, and the goat can give me milk, and the milk is for Oum Bsisi, and she will in return give me back my tail, so I can play with my friends on the morning of Eid."

The butcher said, "Well, little mouse, I need a new knife, go to the blacksmith, and tell him the butcher needs a new knife."

So, off went the mouse to find the blacksmith. "Oh, Mr. Blacksmith, can you please make me a new knife for the butcher so he can give me meat for the dog and her puppies, so they can help the shepherd take care of his sheep? And the shepherd will give me a lamb, and the lamb is for the Ululators, the Ulutators will ululate for the valley, and the valley will give me water, and the water is for the Sidra tree, and the Sidra tree would give me some Nabaq fruit, and the Nabaq is for the goat, and the goat can give me milk, and the milk is for Oum Bsisi, and she will in return give me back my tail, so I can play with my friends on the morning of Eid."

"Well, of course," said the blacksmith. "However, I don't have a strong fire to make a knife. Would you go to the lumberjack, and ask him for some wood to strengthen my fire?"

So, off went the mouse to find the lumberjack.

"Mr. Lumberjack, it has been a long journey for me, would you please help me out with some wood? I need it for the blacksmith, so he can make a stronger fire, to make a knife to give it to the butcher, and so the butcher can give me meat for the dog and her puppies, so they can help the shepherd, to take care of his sheep, and the shepherd will give me a lamb, and the lamb is for the Ululators, and the Ulutators will ululate for the rains to stream the valley, and the valley will give me water, and the water is for the Sidra tree, and the Sidra tree would give me some Nabaq fruit, and the Nabaq is for the goat, and the goat can give me milk, and the milk is for Oum Bsisi, and she will in return give me back my tail, so I can play with my friends on the morning of Eid."

f course, little mouse, how about you go over the hill, and you ask my wife to lend you our donkey to help you carry the wood?" the lumberjack said.

Finally, off went the mouse, he kindly asked the wife for the donkey, and she generously agreed.

Riding the donkey, the mouse went to find the blacksmith, carrying the wood from the lumberjack and his wife. The blacksmith made a new knife and off went the mouse.

The mouse took the knife to the butcher, who cut off some meat for him, to take to the dog and her puppies, who then went to help the shepherd take care of his sheep.

The shepherd gave the Ululators a lamb, and the Ululators ululated over the valley.
The valley gave water to the Sidra tree, and the tree gave some Nabaq fruit for the goat to eat.
The goat gave the little mouse milk, and the little mouse took the milk to Oum Bsisi.
And Oum Bsisi returned his tail.

Excitedly, the mouse ran back to his mother.

"Mother, Mother, Oum Bsisi gave me my tail back!"

And his mother attached his tail.
Then the little mouse went to bed. On the morning of Eid, the mouse was happy, playing with his friends and his little tail!

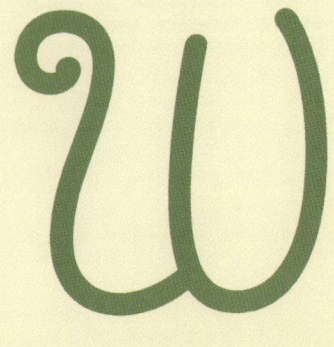hat is the lesson of this story?

What is your favorite character?

What is the new thing that you learned from this story?

From the memory

Printed in Great Britain
by Amazon